Fearless Flynn
and other tales

Contents

Illustrated by T.S. Spookytooth, Fernando Juarez and C.B. Canga

Collins

Fearless Flynn

by Geraldine McCaughrean

One frozen night, when snow had turned the trees into bony fingers, three skeletons lay in ambush by a road. One was small, one was bigger, but the third was huge. (It is a wonder there was ever a body big enough to hold such big and bulky bones.) Nearby, a skeleton horse grazed on stones and twigs and snail shells.

"I hear someone coming," said the first ambusher. "By morning there will be one more skeleton to keep us company!"

"And look! He's only a little fellow," said the second. "One sight of me and the heart will jump clean out of him!"

"And if it does not, we shall win the bones of his skin," said the third.

Along came Flynn, bowling a hoop by his side. Out jumped the first skeleton, rattling his bones like knitting needles. He had a hoop, too.

"Beware, because I've come, Flynn,
To win from you your skin, Flynn!
Play bowl-the-hoop: if I win –
*   You're MINE!"*

But Flynn did *not* jump out of his skin. He did not even scream or try to run away.

"I will play bowl-the-hoop with you," he said, "but I'm afraid you won't like it."

The skeleton grinned back at him. (Well, skeletons cannot help grinning, whether they are happy or not.)

"Begin, Flynn."

Grabbing the skeleton by neck and ankle, Flynn looped it round into a big hoop. One long leg bone he kept back, to use as a stick. Then he bowled the skeleton down the road, up to the top of a hill and down the other side. Faster and faster, bouncing over stones and into pot holes, the skeleton rolled – SPLASH! – right into a freezing pond.

The moon rose up just then, white like a frightened face. Out jumped the second skeleton, bigger than the first.

"*Beware, because I've come, Flynn,*

*To **dance** you out of your skin, Flynn!*"

But Flynn didn't tremble or faint. He didn't even turn pale. "I only dance with ladies," he said.

"I AM a lady!" shrieked the skeleton, most put out. With bony fingers she flicked the red ribbons that fluttered from her neck bone.

"Oh! So sorry," said Flynn. "It's hard to tell with skeletons ... But how can we dance without music?"

The skeleton grinned at Flynn. (Well, skeletons cannot help grinning, whether they are happy or hungry or angry.) Her yellow teeth glinted in the moonlight.

"I shall hum you a tune so we can begin, Flynn," she said.

And she began to yowl and howl and hoo-whooo and to whistle and wail like the wind. It was a fearful sound.

Flynn put his fingers in his ears. "What kind of tune do you call that, lady? I like my music with a good beat!"

And grabbing the skeleton's arm bone, he used it for a drumstick to bang on her hollow head – *Bop! Bop! Bop!* – and then on her yellow teeth – *Ting! Ting! Ting!*

I tell you, he played that skeleton like a xylophone, and while he did, he danced. The bare trees clicked their twiggy fingers. The badgers boogied.

But I don't think the skeleton liked Flynn's music, for bit by bit she went all to pieces.

Suddenly, a giant shape blotted out the moon. The third skeleton towered over Flynn — a giant of a skeleton, mounted on a skeleton horse as huge as scaffolding. A bony nightmare on a bony mare, he grinned at Flynn. (Well, skeletons cannot help grinning, whether they are happy or hungry, or angry, or hugely horrible.)

Beware, because I've come, Flynn,

To **wrestle** *you out of your skin, Flynn!"*

Flynn stared back, wide-eyed, for a long, long time. Then he said ...

"BOO!"

The big skeleton was so surprised that he fell off his horse with a noise like a whole bag of drumsticks.

"I don't care to wrestle," said Flynn, "but this snow is perfect for sledging."

And grabbing the skeleton's ribs, he built himself a toboggan, with thigh bones for runners and hand bones for holding on.

Then he rode it down the snowy hill from midnight till morning, and only twice fell out on his head.

When he picked himself up the second time, the skeleton horse was standing over him, half as high as a hill, looking down with empty, oval eyes, and chewing on chips of ice.

Its hoof scraped the snowy ground. Its yellow teeth
nipped the collar of Flynn's jacket and lifted him clear
off the ground.

"*What would you say to*
a thing, Flynn,

Who can **trample** *you*
out of your skin, Flynn?"

And it reared up,
its horseshoes clipping
the moon.

"I'd say ... 'Have a sugar
lump!'" declared Flynn, reaching
into his pocket.

"In that case," said the horse, "you are the master
for me." And he set Flynn back on his feet.

Flynn took the ribbons from the lady skeleton and
made reins — and the horse pulled his toboggan, all the
way home.

The hoof prints left in the snow were as big as
bowling hoops.

Well, Flynn's story soon got about.

People said, "Flynn is fearless! There goes
Fearless Flynn!"

He never tired of telling the story and people never tired of listening. They would pat him on the back as he helped himself to sugar lumps and say, "Here's to Fearless Flynn!"

One evening, down at the inn, they asked him, "Flynn! Does nothing scare you?"

"Nothing!" he boasted, flinging wide his arms. "Nothing, no how, never!"

His hand brushed a cobweb, and a tiny spider fell on to his sleeve. His face turned as white as a sugar lump and his teeth chattered and his knees knocked and both his socks fell down.

"*Eeek! Get it off! Arghh! Help! Mummy!*"

A little girl had to take the spider away on her fingertip, saying, "It's safe to open your eyes now, Fearless Flynn."

Tom's Shadow Dance

by Martin Waddell

Chapter 1

This is the strange story of Barrel Tom and the shadows. It happened one night when the full moon shone down on the yard of an inn called The Saracen's Head, although some say it never happened at all. Well, *maybe* they are right – or maybe this story is true.

Barrel Tom was a beggar boy, half-starved and thin and he slept on old straw laid in a broken barrel behind the inn. Some days he ate nothing at all and some days Alice who served at the inn brought him scraps, if she could. That is why Tom called her his Alice. He loved her, but he was too shy to say so.

How could a pretty, spirited girl like Alice love a poor boy who lived in a barrel?

On the night that this story begins the inn was a place full of rumpus and joy, for Luke the Blind Fiddler had come with his fiddle. Luke made toes tap with his jigs and there was some magic thing in his music that set people dancing whenever he played.

Slim Sal, Big Waldo the Miller, Owen the Rhymer, Tall Thomas the Tailor and Samsam the Sailor had all taken rooms at the inn and they danced with the villagers while Luke played. They all were good folk, more or less, though some less than more. Alice fetched them this and that. The music made her feet tap and she longed to join in, but she was paid to work, not to dance.

When Luke the Blind Fiddler laid down his bow the villagers wandered off home, still toe-tapping, but the guests at the inn sat by the fire and told stories until they were too tired to talk any more. Then they wished each other "Good night" and "Sleep well" and went off to bed yawning and scratching their heads.

No one spared a thought for poor Barrel Tom shivering outside in the cold … no one but Alice and she couldn't leave to see how Tom was (though she wanted to go) because she had to clear up the mess.

When Alice had finished, she lay down on her trestle bed in the kitchen and fell asleep, for she had to be first up the next morning. It was too late to go out to Barrel Tom for she thought that he would be fast asleep.

But he wasn't.

The night was icy cold and the inn was still. There wasn't a noise to be heard in the yard, as the moonlight shone down on the dark cobblestones turning them silvery white. Barrel Tom lay curled in the straw in his barrel, not sleeping.

Then ... something stirred in the night. Not some*thing*, but some *things*. One after the other, dark shadows came slipping out of the inn. They gathered in the yard on the dark-cobblestones-turned-silvery-white by the light of the moon.

Slim Sal, Big Waldo the Miller, Samsam the Sailor, Tall Thomas the Tailor, Owen the Rhymer, Luke the Blind Fiddler and Kind Alice were *there* and were *not*. It was shadows that came from the inn, not people, for the people were tucked up in bed dreaming and snoring.

There was a faint noise like a tin whistle, just once, and the next sound was the scrape of a fiddle, playing slow notes at first and building up into a jig.

Inside his barrel, Tom couldn't see anything, though he heard the sound of the fiddle. He thought it might be the wind in the rafters, but the wind has no fiddle to play, so he didn't know what it could be. And anyway the night was still, so there was no wind that could play in the rafters.

The music played softly at first as the fiddler picked out the tune. Then it grew wilder and wilder.

Tom's mind filled with the sound of the fiddle and he tapped his feet on the side of his barrel. The music fiddled his brain, till at last Barrel Tom crept out ... at least *part* of Tom did, but he left his shadow behind, asleep.

Out in the yard, Tom couldn't *believe* what he saw, because what he saw just *couldn't* be.

22

Dark shadows danced in the yard of the inn, on the white silvery cobbles lit by the light of the moon. And although he was weary and tired and aching for food, Tom's feet were tapping even faster. He couldn't resist the sound of the fiddle.

Then Barrel Tom found himself dancing, although all of the people he danced with were shadows. Slim Sal, Big Waldo the Miller, Samsam the Sailor, Tall Thomas the Tailor, Owen the Rhymer, Luke the Blind Fiddler and even Kind Alice ... all slept in their rooms, just like Tom's shadow asleep in his barrel. None of them heard the strange tune that was played on a fiddle outside in the yard.

The shadows danced on and on, on and on ... but sometime and somehow, the shadow dance had to end and end it did. The moon that hung over The Saracen's Head was clouded by night and as the light fled the shadow dance finished.

The scrape of a fiddle bow faded away, and suddenly all of the shadows were gone. The only one left dancing was poor Barrel Tom, picking his steps by the sounds that still played in his head.

Barrel Tom danced on and on, on and on.

He danced until at last he grew too weak to dance any more. His head seemed to spin and he fell to the ground. Barrel Tom lay on the dark cobblestones cold and still as though he were dead.

Morning came. The bright light of the sun made the dark cobblestones shine like gold, but poor Tom never stirred.

Chapter 2

The people rose from their sleep and came into the yard, one by one, all but Alice. She was too busy laying the fire, making the beds and preparing food for the guests. She still had a thousand and one things to do before she could think of her Tom and the scraps she had saved for his food.

Out came Slim Sal, Big Waldo the Miller, Samsam the Sailor, Tall Thomas the Tailor, Owen the Rhymer and Luke the Blind Fiddler, stretching themselves in the sunlight.

Then they saw Tom.

"Barrel Tom is lying here!" Owen gasped.

"Wake up!" said Slim Sal.

"He can't wake up. He's dead!" said Big Waldo the Miller.

Everyone was upset and frightened and the sound of their voices reached Alice, who ran out to see what was happening and saw Tom on the ground.

"Tom!" Alice gasped, and she started to cry, as if her poor heart was breaking inside her.

"What's dead is dead, girl!" Tall Thomas the Tailor said sharply.

Alice still wept, though her grief didn't change things one bit. But then *something* happened.

Luke the Blind Fiddler took up his bow, looking bothered and strange. He scraped a few notes slowly, as though he was recalling a tune he had once heard, though he didn't know when or how he had heard it before. Then he stopped, and he frowned, and he started again.

This time Luke played a wild jig as fast as his fiddle could fiddle. He didn't know what note came next, but the notes followed quickly, one after another, as though his fiddle knew just what to play. It was as if Luke's fiddle was playing itself, with no help from Luke.

Something stirred the straw in the barrel, and shivered awake, disturbed by the notes of the strange, wild tune. It was Tom's shadow. It tapped its soft feet on the side of the barrel, with never a sound and then it slipped out of the barrel, looking for Tom.

Out in the yard, over the cold cobblestones, Tom's shadow danced. It danced in the sunlight towards Tom.

And then, once again, Tom and his shadow were one. As Tom's shadow slipped into Tom, poor Tom stirred and started to breathe, and came back to life.

With his shadow inside him, Tom rose and he danced a fantastical dance like no one before him or since. Everyone shouted and clapped and his Alice cried again though this time she was crying for joy.

"We'll call him Tom Dance after this," said Owen the Rhymer. And so it was. Tom stayed Tom Dance for the rest of his days and his dancing was so marvellous and strange that it made him rich and famous. Tom danced round the world and then he came home and married his Alice.

Some say Tom fainted that night for lack of good food and was found in the yard fast asleep. But Tom says that he danced with shadows on silvery white cobblestones to a tune that was played by a blind fiddler's shadow under the light of the moon.

Maybe he did. Maybe this story is true.

Thirteen Crows
by Gillian Shields

Chapter 1

There was a boy called Peter, who lived in a cottage on the edge of a forest. He was a bold, brave lad, but he was made to do all the work by his three idle step-brothers. Their names were Gunter, Gore and Grym and they were the meanest, greediest lumps to be found on this side of the mountains. Gunter was cross-eyed and bow-legged, Gore had a scrawny long face like a donkey, and Grym was as podgy as an over-stuffed turkey.

The village folk sighed to see Peter chop the wood and feed the pigs and scrub the floors, and wondered that he did not grow bitter. But Peter had a rare gift which kept his heart green and growing. It was this. He could carve a bit of wood from the forest into a whistle or pipe, and when he blew, he made such music that even the birds in the trees stopped to listen. His brothers jeered at him and broke his carvings, but Peter kept hope alive in his heart by dreaming that one day he would fill the forest with music.

Not far from the tumbledown cottage was a fine house made of stone. It had high walls round the garden like a prison and tall gates like iron lace. No one ever came in or out of the house. Some folk said that the old man who lived there was a miser, with sacks of gold hidden under his bed. Others said he was mad, or even, it was whispered with a thrill, a murderer.

One day, Peter passed the house on his way to collect firewood and saw the face of an old man at the window. It seemed to Peter that the man was not mad, or wicked, but as sad as a blasted tree that could not grow.

That night, Peter dreamt a strange dream.

In his dream, the old man was drowning in a lake full of dark weeds, and Peter was trying to save him. As he reached out to grasp the man's hand, thirteen black crows beat their wings around Peter's head. The darkness of  their feathers and the stench of death began to smother him. Then Peter cried out in his sleep, until Gunter threw an old boot at him, and Gore snarled, "Shut up, you little rat," and Grym dragged his lumbering carcass out of bed to give the boy a good thump.

Chapter 2

Soon afterwards, the man who lived in the stone house died. Some folk said it was a fever that had killed him, some said a broken heart and others whispered, with a shiver of delight, that he had hanged himself in the cellar. But whatever the truth of it, he was certainly dead, and no one came to attend the funeral.

Did I say that no one came? That wasn't quite true. Thirteen ragged crows appeared from the distant sky and circled the grave, like an omen of evil tidings. Afterwards they settled on the roof of the stone house and Peter remembered the crows from his dream, but said nothing.

The stone house was shut up, the iron gates were locked and weeds rampaged through the gardens. Those thirteen crows still kept guard over the house. Folk said that the place must be haunted, and rumours sprang up thicker than weeds. It was told again and again, with a quiver of excitement, how there was a great stash of gold hidden in the house, left behind for anyone who was brave enough to go and find it.

One night, Gunter, Gore and Grym were sitting round the table in the cottage, chewing over the rumours like dogs with a favourite bone. Their thick heads were on fire with the thought of gold.

"They say there are buckets and buckets of money lying around in that old house," belched Gunter, crashing his fist down on the table.

"They also say the house is haunted," squeaked Gore in fright. "I'm not setting foot in there."

"But I know someone who is," winked Grym. "Boy! BOY!"

The three great puddings lurched to their feet. Gunter grabbed an axe and Gore grabbed Peter and they all stumbled down the lane that led to the old stone house.

When they reached the locked gate, everything was silent in the overgrown garden and the deserted house. Except, that is, for the rustling of the crows' wings, as they perched on the roof in the moonlight.

Gunter swung his axe a mighty blow, smashing the chains on the gate. The gate creaked open and the crows rose up from the roof, flapping their wings in a sudden clamour.

The step-brothers were sweating with fear, but they gripped Peter tightly and pointed at the house. "That little window's just your size. Get in there and get that gold, or we'll skin you alive, so we will!" And they shoved him down the path, with plenty of savage kicks to set him on his way.

Now Peter was a plucky lad, so he squared his shoulders, and quickly squeezed through the half-open window. Inside, all was silent and cold as a grave, lit only by a sliver of moonlight.

It was a sad, forlorn place, and Peter thought with pity of the old man who had spent his lonely days there. He crept from room to room, opening doors, glancing at the shrouded furniture. But there was no sign of any money, not even a brass farthing. Peter was on the point of giving up, when he came upon a locked door.

Peter rattled the handle of the door in vain. Then he remembered seeing a heavy iron key in the old man's bedroom, hanging on a black ribbon by the gloomy four poster bed. Peter ran lightly to fetch it, and fitted the strangely decorated key into the lock.

As Peter pushed the door open, he saw an empty room.

A lamp hanging from the ceiling flickered with an eerie light. On the floor was a single iron chest. As in a dream, Peter lifted up the heavy lid, and gasped. The chest was crammed with gold coins of every shape and size, shimmering like honey in the lamplight.

On top of the coins was a small book, bound in soft leather. Peter picked it up and read where it fell open at the first page.

"To those who seek their fortune – beware! This gold brings only death and despair to those who touch it. Mad they called me, and a miser, but I have kept these cursed coins away from human sight, to stop any poor unfortunate soul coming into contact with them ..."

Peter dropped the book in horror and at that moment, he seemed to hear the crows screeching to each other, as though the dark room was full of flapping, cawing birds. He turned and ran like a hare back to his brothers, who were waiting impatiently at the gate.

"I've found the gold," he panted, "but you mustn't touch it!"

"Don't touch it?" roared Grym. "I'd like to see you stop me!"

"But there's a warning ..." began Peter.

"... And I'm warning you that if you don't go and fetch that gold, I'll knock your head off," threatened Grym.

But nothing could persuade Peter to go and get a single coin, not even blows. So, with much grumbling and cursing, the step-brothers drew lots to see which one of them should fetch the gold.

Chapter 3

The task fell to the unlucky, lanky Gore, which was fortunate for the brothers, as neither Gunter nor Grym would ever have got through the narrow window. But at last Gore managed it. Trembling from head to toe, he found his way to the room with the iron chest. The book he tossed aside, as he had never bothered to learn to read, and he fell greedily upon the glowing coins. The chest was too heavy for him to lift, so he crammed his pockets with as much gold as he could carry, before scuttling out of there like a frightened beetle.

Back at the cottage, Gore, Grym and Gunter divided the gold coins into three piles, squabbling and fighting as they did so, as none of those fine turnip heads could count quite perfectly.

At last they were satisfied with their shares. And at the bottom of Gore's pocket, they found a single copper penny, which he had mistaken for gold in his haste.

"That's for you, little brother," they jeered. Throwing the penny at Peter, they laughed and slapped their thighs at the thought of all the things they could buy in the morning. But Peter sat in a corner, eyeing the copper coin fearfully as he turned it in his hands.

As soon as it was light, the step-brothers hurried off to the distant market town, jingling the money in their pockets.

Gunter, who loved nothing better than killing small creatures in the forest, bought traps and whips and daggers and knives. Gore, who flattered himself that he was a handsome fellow, chose a fine new suit of satin with a real silk neckerchief. He also bought a fiery chestnut horse, so that he could swagger round the village in grand style. Grym, who loved his belly above everything, spent his money on hams and geese and mutton, and an enormous peacock pie.

The next day, the brothers were bent upon enjoying their purchases. Gunter hurried out to set his traps in the forest. Gore dressed up in his finery (though he didn't bother to wash first) and galloped off. He bounced around on the saddle, whipping the unfortunate horse with a flourish. Only Grym stayed behind, to prepare a gigantic feast for himself.

Grym ordered Peter about all day long, shouting, "Boy! Fetch me a sharp knife!" and "Stoke up the fire!"

When the table was at last groaning with food, he attacked it greedily, guzzling and gorging and smacking his lips. Stuffing a whole sausage into his mouth, Grym mumbled, "Bring me that pie, boy ... oy ... oh ... aaah!"

He began to cough, then choke, then turn purple in the face. Clutching his neck, Grym stumbled out into the yard, gasping for breath. Peter ran in alarm after him, just in time to see him fall down dead upon the ground – crash! – the sausage still stuck in his throat.

At that moment, Gore rode towards the cottage on his sweating horse, his fine clothes crumpled from hard riding.

"Grym!" he yelled, when he saw his brother lying stretched out in the yard. "What's wrong?"

Gore whipped his horse savagely to go faster, but the startled creature reared up in surprise and pain and shot wildly into the forest.

Terrified, Gore clung on, but his fluttering silken
neckerchief became caught in the branches and – snap! –
his neck was broken in an instant. His body hung from the
tree like a common thief on the gallows.

Peter could only watch helplessly as the horse bucked
and shied and galloped amongst the trees, where Gunter
was walking home after his day's hunt.

Gunter was pulling a string of dead rabbits behind him, when he looked up with fear, as the maddened horse trampled him down.

He fell backwards into one of his own pits, where – crunch! – the spikes of a trap killed him instantly. Peter was dumb with shock and horror, for it is not a cheering sight to see your step-brothers drop down dead all at once, however mean or lazy they have been when alive.

At that moment, Peter heard the sound of crows calling to each other. He looked up and there they were, thirteen black shadows circling in the dusk. His heart trembled with fear at the thought that the cursed gold had caused his brothers' terrible deaths. Snatching up the copper penny, Peter ran without stopping to the old stone house.

The thirteen crows flew after him, as swift as a storm. He scrambled into the house and up the stairs.

"I don't want it," Peter cried to the silent rooms. "I don't want your money, whoever you are! Take it back!" He threw himself into the room where he had found the money and scrabbled to find the book, desperate to read and know more. He snatched it with trembling hands and read the pages where they fell open.

"*When you read this, I shall be dead and my spirit will be at peace at last,*" it said. "*I lived in this house in my former life. Ah! What a sorrowful house it is, and what a strange and terrible tale I have to tell!*

"*Many years ago, an old woman lived alone in this house, hoarding her money. The only living things she loved were her thirteen tame crows. My grandfather was a greedy man, alas, and he took advantage of her lonely state. He trapped and killed the crows, and cheated her of her gold. How my family has paid for this crime! For before she died, the old woman cursed the money so that no good can come to anyone who touches even one penny of it, only death.*"

Peter gazed at the copper penny in his hand with frightened eyes, then read on.

"*If you don't believe me, know that my grandfather and father both met death before their natural time. So when this dread inheritance came to me, I did what I could to keep the cursed coins untouched by man or woman. They are all tainted with evil.*"

"So what can I do?" said Peter wildly to himself as he read on.

"*If you, who have now found the hoard, try to spend the coins, or even give them to another, be warned that death will seek you out.*

"*There is only one way to break free. You must find some way of doing good with the money – without spending it, or giving it away. How often have I groaned over this impossible task! If like me, you cannot solve this cursed riddle, you must shut yourself away with your accursed wealth and live a life like mine, alone and lonely as a withered tree. But if you have already touched the money, it is too late! Prepare yourself for death ...*"

Chapter 4

Peter threw the book away and ran to and fro crying out,
"What shall I do with the copper penny? I cannot spend
it, and I cannot give it away. I must solve the riddle!
Yet what good can a poor boy like me do in this
great world?"

Then he sank down in despair, while the dark hours of
night raced by. But as he sat huddled and wretched in the
cold stone house, his brave young heart refused to give up.
It seemed to Peter that he heard a few notes of a sweet
melody playing in his head.

"The only good thing I know is my music," he thought,
and he looked up with something like hope in his eyes.

Clasping the copper penny in his hand, Peter stood up and locked the door of the hateful room behind him. He carefully replaced the key on the hook in the old man's bedroom, hanging on its black ribbon. Then he left the dark house, ran down the track to the sleeping village and slipped quietly into the blacksmith's forge.

Sneaking through the window, Peter laid the copper penny on the great anvil and began to beat it with a strong hammer. He beat that penny until the sweat ran down his face and the copper became smooth and flat like pastry under a rolling pin. Then he curled the thin sheet of metal into a little whistle. It was the finest whistle Peter had ever made.

It was nearly dawn, so Peter went out into the middle of the village and began to play. His music rose up to the morning star like the lark's song, like the murmur of crystal waterfalls, like the voice of the angels.

All the villagers woke from their sleep and went out in their nightshirts and as the sun climbed up into the sky, even the deer and the badgers and foxes crept from the forest to listen and wonder.

48